MW01048844

STOP THAT TRAIN!

By Ace Landers
Illustrated by Sean Wang

SCHOLASTIC INC.

ISBN 978-1-338-26053-3

10 9 8 7 6 5 4 3 2   18 19 20 21 22

Printed in the U.S.A. 40

First printing 2018

Book design by Mercedes Padró

One day, a young man rushes through LEGO® City to catch his train.

3

The trains in LEGO City always run on time. Usually that's a good thing—but not today! If he's late to the station, his train might leave without him.

Nothing is going to get in his way—not even the delicious smells coming from the pizza truck. There's no time for pepperoni today!

It's peak travel time in LEGO City. Everyone is getting out of work and ready to have fun—or go home and change into their fuzzy slippers.

A driver for a passenger train watches the clock. He makes sure that travel runs smoothly. "All aboard!" he announces at five o'clock sharp. The train pulls away from the station.

"Wait!" the man yells, but it's too late!

Just outside the station there is a cargo train about to leave. It's heading in the same direction that the man wants to go!

The man runs over and flags down the driver. "Please, I missed my train and I need to get somewhere right away," the man says. "Can I get a ride with you?"

The driver nods. "Okay, but you'll have to ride with the crew."

The crew does not look thrilled at having to fit one more.

As the cargo train leaves the station, the man checks his watch. Everything is back on track . . .

The man can tell that he's going to be late if he doesn't do something now. He finds a pair of binoculars and spots the passenger train from earlier stopped at a station off in the distance!

It's now or never. He runs as fast as he can toward the station. He makes it on the train just as the doors close behind him and waves his ticket in the air. "I made it! I made it!" he cheers and everybody claps.

The man takes the last open seat. Phew! It isn't long before the driver makes an announcement. "Ladies and gentlemen, we have reached our final destination. Thank you for riding with us."

The man leaves the station and rushes to a nearby house, hoping that he isn't too late. The house is dark and it looks like no one is home. He opens the front door.

"SURPRISE!"

A bright light turns on and a crowd of people suddenly jump out from behind doorways and furniture, shouting and waving their arms.

He made it to the surprise party on time! But the surprise isn't for him. He turns off the lights and everyone hides again, waiting for the real guest of honor.

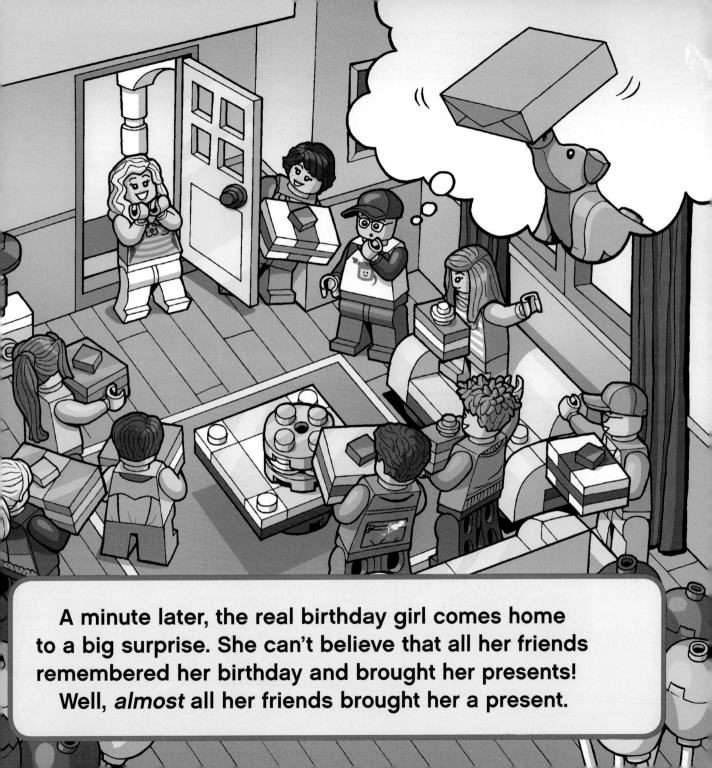

A minute later, the real birthday girl comes home to a big surprise. She can't believe that all her friends remembered her birthday and brought her presents! Well, *almost* all her friends brought her a present.

"I promise I had a present for you," the man tells his friend. "Let's just say your birthday gift is that I even made it to this party at all!"